Adapted from *The Brothers Grimm*
by Eric A. Kimmel

The Four Gallant Sisters

Illustrated by Tatyana Yuditskaya

Henry Holt and Company · New York

To Susan Fletcher
—E. A. K.

To all my teachers
—T. Y.

Text copyright © 1992 by Eric A. Kimmel
Illustrations copyright © 1992 by Tatyana Yuditskaya
First edition
Published by Henry Holt and Company, Inc.,
115 West 18th Street, New York, New York 10011.
Published simultaneously in Canada by Fitzhenry & Whiteside Ltd.,
195 Allstate Parkway, Markham, Ontario L3R 4T8.

Library of Congress Cataloging-in-Publication Data
Kimmel, Eric A.
The four gallant sisters / adapted from the Brothers Grimm
by Eric A. Kimmel; illustrated by Tatyana Yuditskaya.
Summary: A variation of two tales from the Brothers Grimm,
in which four orphaned sisters disguise themselves as men
to go out in the world and learn a trade.
ISBN 0-8050-1901-4 (acid-free paper)
[1. Fairy tales.   2. Folklore—Germany.]
I. Yuditskaya, Tatyana, ill.   II. Title.
PZ8.K527Fo   1992   398.21′0941—dc20
[E]   91-28231

Henry Holt books are available at special discounts
for bulk purchases for sales promotions, premiums,
fund-raising, or educational use. Special editions
or book excerpts can also be created to specification.

Printed in the United States of America
on acid-free paper. ∞

10   9   8   7   6   5   4   3   2   1

Once upon a time, four sisters lived with their ailing mother. When their mother died, the oldest sister said to the others, "We are alone now with no one to look after us. We must make our own way in the world, no easy task, and doubly hard for women. I propose that we disguise ourselves as men and learn a trade. That way we can provide for ourselves and not be dependent on anyone."

The sisters cut off their long hair. They put away their dresses and attired themselves in men's clothing. Then, after promising to meet by their mother's grave in seven years, they set out into the wide world to find whatever fortune awaited them.

The oldest sister had not gone far when she met a tailor. "You strike me as being a lad with a taste for fine clothes," the tailor exclaimed. "How would you like to learn the tailor's trade?"

"I think not," said the oldest sister. "Tailors are as common as dandelions. Besides, I see no great skill in sewing pieces of cloth together."

"Oho! Is that what you think?" the tailor replied. "Let me tell you, my lad, if not for tailors, people would go naked as Adam and Eve. We tailors hold the key to greatness. A few yards of velvet, a spray of lace, tucked here, pleated there, and lo—a peasant becomes a prince! I tell you, no finer trade exists. Become a tailor and your fortune is assured."

Intrigued by this promise, the oldest sister apprenticed herself to the tailor. For seven years she studied the tailor's art, becoming as skilled a tailor as ever pulled thread. At the end of her apprenticeship, her master gave her a parting gift: a needle that could sew anything, from chain mail to gossamer, with a seam so fine as to be invisible.

The second sister wandered through the countryside. Along the way she fell in with a huntsman. He judged her a likely lad and asked if she cared to learn the hunter's trade.

"I think not," the second sister answered. "A hunter's life is hard and lonely."

The huntsman replied, "One man's burden is another's joy. To drink clear water from a spring; to sleep on a bed of ferns beneath a sky alive with stars; to feel the wind's kiss before dawn on a winter morning: city folk would call it a hard life. And lonely. But I would no more trade my lot for theirs than a hawk would trade places with a chicken. Come with me, lad, and learn what it means to really live. I will teach you the ways of the forest. I will show you where the mushrooms grow, where the salmon come to spawn, where the she-bear digs her den. You will learn to track, to hunt, to bring down your quarry with one sure shot. The boar will be your companion. The stag will call you brother."

Captivated by these words, the second sister apprenticed herself to the huntsman. For seven years she roamed the forest, unveiling its secrets one by one until nothing in nature remained hidden from her. When her apprenticeship ended, she too received a parting gift: a gun that never missed its mark.

The third sister stopped at a village fair. Among the performers she saw a man who called himself a finger artist. For a time he strolled unnoticed through the fairgoers. Then he called for attention and held up watches, rings, and purses which he returned to their astonished owners. "Thief!" some shouted. But the man replied, "Does a thief ever return what he steals? I am no thief. I am a finger artist, a master of sleight of hand. Allow me to demonstrate my skill."

And so he did! He removed an unsuspecting soldier's boots and buttons. He stole one man's glass eye and another's wooden hand. He switched two babies, swaddling clothes and all, without their mothers' being aware. It was a masterful performance.

When he had finished, the third sister ran up to him. "I wish to learn a trade. Nothing would please me more than to become a finger artist."

"It is not easy, for it requires much practice," the man told her. "Furthermore, these skills are dangerous in the wrong hands. You must swear yourself to total honesty."

"I do!" the third sister replied without hesitation.

And so the finger artist accepted her as his apprentice. By the end of seven years she had surpassed her master, becoming so skilled at the art of sleight of hand she could unravel a spider's web and weave it back together without disturbing the spider. At the end of her apprenticeship, her master presented her with a parting gift: a magic belt that had the power to make the wearer invisible.

As for the fourth sister, she traveled on until she came to a tall tower. A stargazer stood at the top of that tower, gazing at the sky through a telescope.

"Where are you going, young scholar?" he called down.

"I seek to learn a trade to earn my fortune," the fourth sister told him.

"Heavens be praised!" the stargazer cried. "My reading of the stars foretold that on this day a young scholar would arrive to study the stargazer's art with me. In seven years' time he will become the greatest stargazer of all. You, my friend, are the one the stars predicted."

The prophecy came true. The youngest sister remained in the tower for seven years. In that time she became the greatest stargazer who ever scanned the heavens. At the end of her apprenticeship, her master too presented her with a parting gift: a telescope from which nothing was hidden.

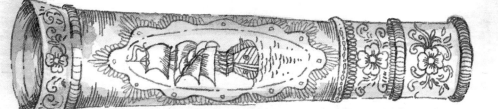

The four sisters returned home. Each had grown wise and skilled. The oldest was a master tailor; the second was a master hunter; the third was a finger artist, a master of sleight of hand; and the fourth was a master stargazer. Little remained of their old home. Brambles and briars covered their mother's grave.

"Nothing is left for us here," the oldest sister said. "Where will we go now?"

The second sister replied, "I have heard that the old king is dead. Perhaps the new one will take us into his service."

This was an excellent idea, for then the four sisters could stay together. They traveled to the city, where they presented themselves to the young king and asked to be taken into his service.

"First, you must prove your skills," the king said to the stargazer. "A bronze weather vane stands atop my castle. A stork has built her nest on it. Quickly, tell me how many eggs are in the nest."

The stargazer looked through her telescope. "There are five."

"Can you bring them down without disturbing the mother bird?" the king asked the finger artist.

can." The finger artist buckled the magic belt around her waist. Quick as a cat, she climbed the castle walls until she reached the weather vane. She stole the eggs from the mother bird without ruffling a feather and brought them down without cracking any. The king took the eggs and set them on a table: one egg in each corner, with the fifth one in the middle. He said to the hunter, "Can you split these eggs with one shot?"

"I can." The hunter aimed her gun and split all the eggs neatly in two with a single bullet.

ow, can you sew them back together again?" the king asked the tailor. The tailor took her needle and sewed up the eggs with an invisible seam. The finger artist carried them back to the nest. When the baby storks hatched a few days later, each one had a thin red line around its body, for the tailor had used red thread to sew the eggs together.

The king's satisfaction knew no bounds. He accepted the four sisters as his attendants. But his mother was doubtful.

"Something is wrong here," she told her son. "My instincts tell me your new attendants are women, not men."

"Impossible!" the king exclaimed. "How could women possess such skill?"

"Women possess more skills than you imagine," the king's mother said quietly. "I say they are women, and I can prove it. Set a sideboard with meat and cheese, then invite them to help themselves. If they fill their own plates and no one else's, they are men. However, since they are women and therefore more considerate, I predict they will serve each other first."

Now it so happened that the third sister, the finger artist, was hiding behind the tapestry and overheard the conversation between the king and his mother. She warned her sisters at once.

"When the king invites us to help ourselves, we must make certain to fill our own plates and no one else's. The king's mother suspects we are women."

"Yet if we all do that, she will be equally suspicious," the youngest sister, the stargazer, said. "People are as different as the stars in the heavens, and women and men never behave entirely one way or another. I propose we take small portions, returning to the sideboard several times, sometimes to fill our own plates, sometimes to serve each other."

"What does that prove?" the second sister, the hunter, asked.

"It proves whatever you like." The oldest sister, the tailor, chuckled.

The king summoned his new attendants to dinner, watching closely while they ate. After dismissing them, he turned to his mother and said, "You see, they are men. They all helped themselves."

"They also served each other, which means they could be women. The test has failed. No matter. We will try again," the king's mother said.

She took a shovelful of ashes from the hearth and sprinkled them in front of the doorway. Then she said to her son, "Call your attendants back. If they walk through the ashes and track soot all over the carpet, they are men. Men never notice these things. But I believe they are women, so I expect them to pause to sweep up the mess."

However, the third sister, the finger artist, had lingered by the door and overheard this conversation too. She went at once to her sisters.

"The king's mother has strewn the floor with ashes. Walk straight on, even if it means tracking soot on the rug. Otherwise, she will know we are women. She believes women are tidier than men."

But the oldest sister, the master tailor, remembered the stargazer sister's words. "That is not always true, but it does give me an idea. Listen to my plan."

When the four sisters came before the king, they walked straight through the ashes, tracking soot on the carpet. The two older sisters, the tailor and the hunter, noticed the mess. They attempted to clean it up, but the result was worse than before. The two younger sisters looked on and did nothing.

"What does this prove?" the king asked his mother.

The king's mother sighed. "It proves they are even cleverer than I suspected. Let it be. We will trouble them no further. My instincts tell me they are women. Time will prove me right."

The next day, a messenger arrived with dreadful news. The young king's promised bride, a beautiful princess, and her four brothers had been kidnapped on their way to the castle for the wedding. A fiery dragon had swooped down from the sky and plucked the princess from the middle of the procession. When her brothers tried to defend her, the dragon picked them up too and flew away—no one knew where!

"Can you find them?" the distraught king asked the stargazer.

The stargazer peered through her telescope. "I see them. The dragon has taken them to a rocky island in the middle of the sea. Give us a ship, and we will rescue them."

The king gave the four sisters a sailing ship. They sailed for seven days. Then the stargazer said, "We are approaching the island. The dragon is asleep. The princess and her four brothers lie helpless in its coils."

The hunter raised her gun, then lowered it. "If I shoot the dragon, it might crush them in its death throes."

"Then I will steal them away," the finger artist said as she buckled on her magic belt. She took the ship's boat and rowed to the island. There she deftly plucked the princess and her four brothers from the dragon's coils. Together, with all possible speed, they rowed back to the ship.

When the dragon awoke and found no trace of the princess or her brothers, it let out a roar. Spewing blasts of fire and smoke, it flew in pursuit of the rescuers. The hunter watched it approach. She waited until the last moment, then raised her gun and fired. The bullet struck the dragon through the heart. It dropped into the sea, raising a giant wave that dashed the ship against the rocks, breaking it to pieces.

"We are lost!" the princess cried.

"Not so!" answered the oldest sister, the master tailor. "I can save us, if you will all help me. Gather together the pieces of the ship. Bring them to me at once."

The four sisters, the four princes, and the princess climbed onto floating planks and paddled through the waves, collecting wood, rope, and canvas.

The second sister and the second prince assembled the fragments of the hull.

The third sister and the third prince collected the masts and spars.

The youngest sister and the youngest prince gathered the sails and rigging. Only the rudder was missing. The princess saw it drifting away and swam after it. Pushing it in front of her while she kicked, she brought it back to the others. Then the oldest sister took her magic needle and, with the help of the oldest prince, sewed the ship together so tightly that not a drop of water seeped between its timbers. Together, they hoisted the sails and set a course for home.

When they arrived, the king greeted them with joy. "Bravo, my gallant men! You have rescued my bride!"

"Gallant as they are, they are women," his mother insisted.

The princess's brothers overheard her. "Women, are they? We wish it were so. We never had truer friends or more valiant companions. If they were women, we would marry them at once."

"And who would you marry?" the princess asked her brothers in turn. They answered without hesitation.

"I would marry the stargazer, who discovered the island," said the youngest prince.

"I would marry the finger artist, who slipped us from the dragon's coils," said the third.

"I would marry the hunter, who slew the dragon with one shot," said the second.

"And I," said the oldest, "would marry the tailor, who sewed our ship together."

"You have chosen your brides, if they will have you," the princess said. She looked at the sisters with a steady gaze.

"We will!" the four gallant sisters exclaimed together.

The king was astonished. "How could you be so sure they were women?" he asked the princess.

"It was simple," she replied with a smile. "Who but women would undertake such trials without demanding a reward?"

A grand wedding took place the next day. The young king married his princess, and the four gallant sisters married her brothers. And they all lived happily ever after. But happiest of all was the king's mother. For she had been right all along.